Patrolman Pete

A Windy Day

AA Published by AA Publishing.

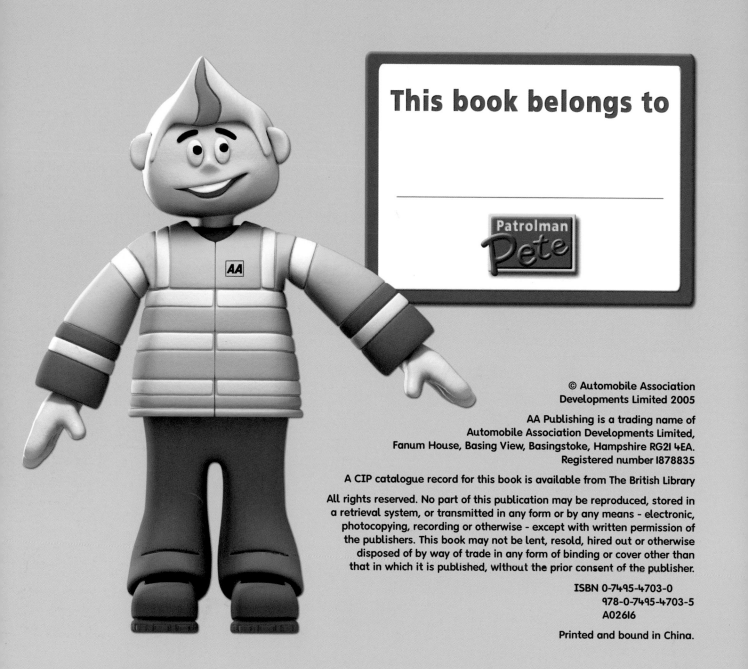

This book belongs to

Patrolman
Pete

© Automobile Association
Developments Limited 2005

AA Publishing is a trading name of
Automobile Association Developments Limited,
Fanum House, Basing View, Basingstoke, Hampshire RG21 4EA.
Registered number 1878835

A CIP catalogue record for this book is available from The British Library

ISBN 0-7495-4703-0
978-0-7495-4703-5
A02616

Printed and bound in China.

A Windy Day

Written by Michelle Hogg

"Ladies and gentlemen," said the mayor. "Hello and…
oh, bother."

The mayor was practising his speech because today was a
very special day. Today he was going to open the Christmas
fair. The problem was that he kept forgetting what to say!

"I know," said the mayor. "I'll write my speech on a piece
of paper. That way I won't forget any of the words."

The mayor fetched a pen and paper and wrote down the words of his speech.

"There," he said, "I won't forget what to say now!"

He put on his coat, then picked up his hat and the speech and set off to the Christmas fair in his big, blue car.

Suddenly there was a loud **BANG!** The mayor's car stopped and, no matter how hard he tried, he couldn't make it start again.

On the other side of town, Patrolman Pete and Trevor the Toolbox were cleaning Stan the Van when they heard Rita from the call centre on the radio.

"Patrolman Pete, Patrolman Pete," she said. "I have a very important job for you. The mayor's car has broken down and he needs your help."

"Righto, Rita, we're ready to roll," shouted Pete, Trevor and Stan together.

It wasn't long before Pete saw the mayor and his big, blue car, so Stan pulled up behind.

"Oh, Pete," cried the mayor, "thank goodness you're here. I was on my way to the Christmas fair, when... Oh, no! My speech!"

The piece of paper the mayor had been holding blew out of his hand and up into the air!

Just at that moment, Mrs Miggins, the postwoman, rode past on her bicycle. "Happy Christmas to you all," she called over her shoulder.

The mayor watched in horror as the piece of paper looped the loop and landed in her basket.

"Mrs Miggins!" shouted Pete, waving his hands. "Stop!"

It was too late. Mrs Miggins didn't hear Pete as she cycled up the hill.

"Oh, dear!" cried the mayor. "Everyone will be waiting at the town square to hear my speech, but now it's lost forever."

"Don't worry!" said Pete. "I know what to do! We'll follow Mrs Miggins, get your speech back and take you to the town square in time to open the Christmas fair."

Pete, Trevor and the mayor jumped aboard Stan and drove up the hill after Mrs Miggins.

"Look!" cried the mayor. "There she is!"

The mayor watched Mrs Miggins reach inside her basket and pull out a handful of letters and... yes, there was the speech!

"Mrs Miggins!" shouted Pete, Trevor, Stan and the mayor together as they drove towards her.

Mrs Miggins was so surprised that she dropped all the letters. The mayor's speech blew up into the air and was carried away once more.

"Oh, no," gasped the mayor. "There goes my speech again."

Trevor stopped to help Mrs Miggins pick up the letters, while Pete, Stan and the mayor chased after the piece of paper.

As they turned into the town square, they ran right into a crowd of people. When the people saw the mayor, they all began to clap and cheer.

"Oh, no!" said the mayor. "Everyone's waiting to hear my speech! Whatever shall I do?"

The poor mayor looked really worried.

The mayor walked up onto the platform and the crowd fell silent.

"Um... ladies and gentlemen," he said. "Um... yes, hello ladies and gentlemen."

No matter how hard he tried, without his speech, he just couldn't remember what to say.

He was wondering what to do next, when suddenly...

"Beep, beep... beep, beep!"

Everyone turned to see what all the noise was about.

"Beep, beep, beep!"

Stan the Van was beeping his horn loudly.

"Look!" shouted Trevor. "Look up there!"

Trevor was pointing to the Christmas tree that stood in the middle of the town square. A small piece of paper was caught on the star right at the very top of the tree.

"Quick," said Pete to Stan and Trevor. "Come with me!"

Stan parked at the bottom of the Christmas tree and stretched out his long arm. "It's no good, Pete," he said. "I can't quite reach."

"Let me help! Let me help!" cried Trevor.

"Alright," said Pete, "but you must be very careful."

When Trevor reached the top of the tree, he carefully stood on tiptoe and grabbed the piece of paper. Once Stan had gently lowered him, Trevor handed the speech to Pete who rushed over to the mayor.

The mayor looked at the paper and then he smiled.

"You've found my speech!" he exclaimed. "Oh, thank you, Pete! Thank you Stan and Trevor, too!"

The mayor cleared his throat and said, "Ladies and gentlemen, I now declare this Christmas fair officially open!"

The lights on the Christmas tree came on, the brass band began to play and everybody cheered!

A Tall Tale

Chaos at the Café

Collect all of the Patrolman Pete adventures!

Stan Gets Wet

A Windy Day